HIDE
to
LIVE
Chilling Tales
by
Aarav Mehta

Published by **Gunjan Publishing House**, Delhi, India.

Ph. No. 8076141973

ISBN: 978-93-342-9563-4

Cover design and book layout by Aarav Mehta

Printed in India

I am Aarav Mehta, a 13-years-old boy of class 8th in Ahlcon Public School situated in Delhi, Mayur Vihar, Phase-1.

It's my first Horror book.

I like to read and make stories through my powerful imaginations.

This book is made because of full support and love from my lovely mother, Adv. Gunjan Mehta and my pillar of strength like father, Adv. Amrendra Kumar Mehta.

I want to become an Advocate of Supreme Court of India, just like my father, and try my best, so that all the poor people can attain their justice.

This book doesn't depict any real incident.

CONTENTS

ZOMBIES INCREASING

Chapter 1
Planned to meet friend's brother

I had planned to meet my old friend's elder brother, who had left India about 3-4 years ago.

He settled in New York where he found a job, He had a marriage ceremony so he had invited me. I booked a flight and packed my bag; my brother also joined me. The flight was of 6 am for the next day.

I bought edibles for the flight and my brother was arranging cloths.

We slept comfortably that night to prevent tiredness in the flight. But in the midnight, I got a message on my phone, about any disease or any infection, I ignored it and kept sleeping.

I woke up early in the morning, at around 4 am and got ready.

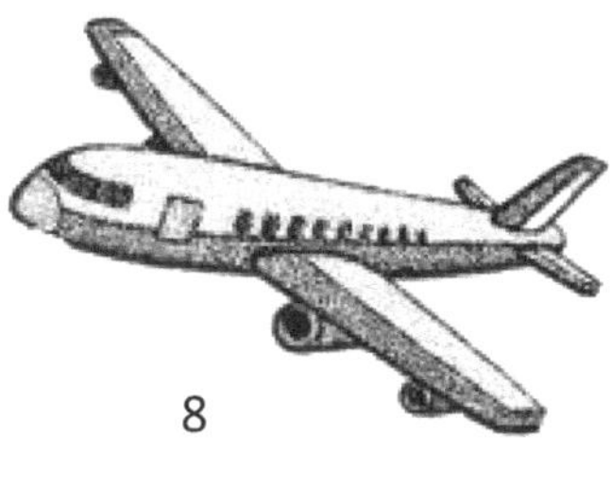

I told my brother to wake up and to get ready, it was around 4:30 am.

He immediately woke up and got ready, it was around 5 am when he was ready.

I made some chapatis for both of us, and booked a taxi, it

came within 10 minutes.

We went inside the taxi with our luggage and the taxi driver took us to the airport.

He helped us to take the luggage till the entry of the airport and then went back.

We went inside the airport, and started finding our flight arrival and it had come, so we went inside the flight, and found our seats, we put our luggage in the shelf and sat on our seat.

My brother had slept…

Chapter 2
In the Flight

After sometime I went to the washroom to wash my face, where I listened a crew screaming that someone was injured; to see that, I also went with her.

I saw a girl lying on the floor.

Her hand was stained with blood, she had a bite on her hand.

I thought some animal must have bitten her outside the flight.

But just after it, unfortunately, she attacked on the crew and the crew also got fainted. Everyone at that place was scared.

Then I remembered about the message that I hadreceived in the midnight.

“Alert: An unidentified communicable disease or infection found in 2 people which make people a living dead, just like a **Zombie**”

Chapter 3
Zombie in the flight

I was scared, so, firstly I locked the door of business class section and ran towards my seat, and told my brother to wake up, then I shouted "quickly take out parachute bags that are put on the shelves, and be ready to jump from the flight because there are zombies in the flight"

As I was sure that no one in the lobby could be able to defend the zombie (the bitten girl), because there were 4 people including me!

Luckily there was a police man in the flight who had a gun... by the shadow of zombies on the translucent glass, I tried to shoot them, but I could shoot only 2 out of 3, the crew and the girl.

But the other one attacked the police man who was in front of me, I immediately pulled the trigger but there were 0 bullets left!!!

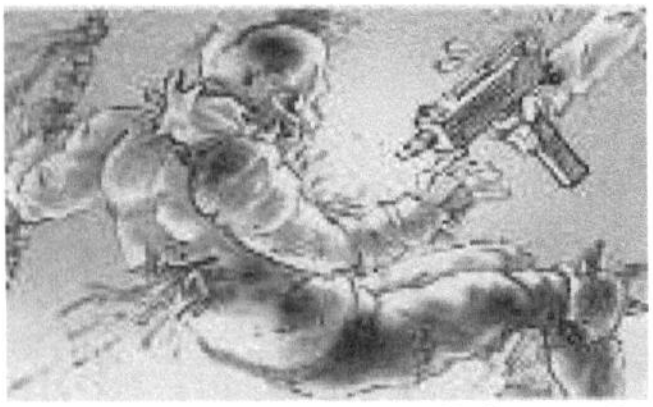

So, I kicked the zombie who had attacked the policeman, and quickly ran towards the pilot.

Before we could go in the pilot's cabin, unfortunately, the plane had landed,
and the zombie I kicked, fell down from the brokenwindow, but the infected police man attacked 3 people beside me!!!
They got infected, and in the plane, there were 90 passengers, out of which 4 were now infected!!

This was the worst time...

We all tried to come out of the small exit of the flight, but it took time, so 11 more got attacked and infected.
Everyone got in a rush. But it was in everyone's luck that who will die and who will live.

My brother always kept my hand in his hand, as he was scared if we both got separated.

The plane had landed near a train station, so everyone preferred to go in any of the trains, so I also went with them.

Only 75 left, and no one knew from where the zombies would occur.

In the way, we saw many zombies, they saw us and ran towards us. There were less hopes of being survived. There were almost 50-60 people already infected there!!

Me and my brother and many other people ran quickly, only 15-16 were left, they safely went to the 6th coach of a

train with my brother and they were safe there.

But me and 2 more people were in the coach no. 2. We had to reach there, but to go there, we had to cross 3 coaches. Which was not easy, because for that, we had to fight with zombies!!

Chapter 4
Fight with zombies!

So, we planned to fight with them…

Out of us, there was a boy, who had many tape rolls with him,

So, we pasted tape on our hands, neck, and legs, for the safety, so that the zombies could not bite us.

We took one rod for each one from the storage area, and took a deep breath then entered in the coach.

I was in the front; the boy was in the middle and the plump man in the back.

We fought with the zombies at that coach; by hitting on head of each of the zombies, we lastly crossed coach no.3.

coach no.4 was empty, but in the 5th coach, there were friends of that boy, he was unable to hit them as he was emotional, but me and the man, without being emotional, started hitting each one at the head.

(! HEAD SHOT !)

We reached the 6th coach's lobby and when I called my brother to open the door of the coach, he opened the door, but a zombie had bitten him!! and the people were not present there.

I was sure, that they all may have got infected.

Chapter 5
Train stopped

Suddenly the train stopped, and the big problem was that, the other people were infected, as I thought, and they were coming towards us.
We had no option, we had to go out of the train, but firstly, I thought that tying my brother's mouth was much important.

I quickly tied a towel tightly around his mouth, so that he could not bite us, and ran outside. The boy was running fast, as he was afraid, but another train came which was filled with zombies and unfortunately hit the boy… the boy was dead and blood was spreading out of hishead!!!

This was unbelievable, and his face was… I cannot talk about that!!

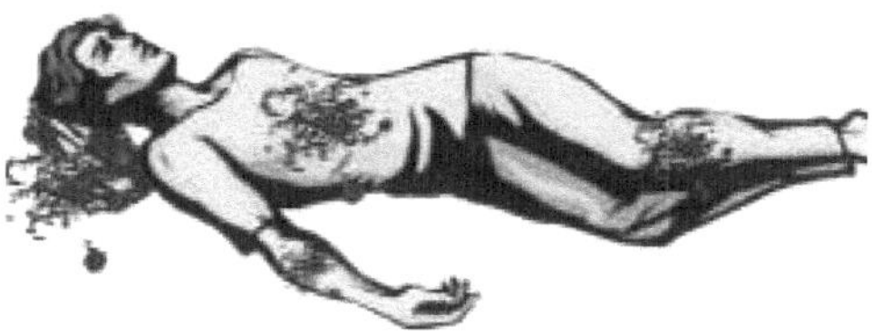

And the other man's leg stuck in the train's bogie.

He was losing his hopes of being survived, he told me to leave. But I was unable to leave him, on the other hand, zombies were coming!

What could I do now!!!

I tried to stretch his leg but he was having pain, just after that, zombies attacked the man!

Beside me was my brother who was unable to bite me as I had tied his mouth.

I was the only one there, not infected!

I quickly picked my brother up on my shoulder and ran as fast I could.

In the way, a girl with a jeep came towards us and told me to sit in the jeep, I could not reject as I was tired and had no stamina.

She told me her name, Adira. So, I

also told my name to her, Aarav...
and added that my brother's name is Aryan, who was infected and sitting behind.

She offered me water, but I said "no", as I could notbelieve on her, as she was a stranger.

I was sure that she was not infected...

We had an advantage of the jeep, that if any zombie occurs, we could hit it without getting bitten by it.

Chapter 6
3 people left

After some time, I saw a temple, and told Adira to stop there.

A picked up my brother on my shoulders and entered the temple.

To check any safe place, I went in a big room, where I saw 50+ big containers, and a pipe attached to it which goes till a river beside the temple.

From the stairs I went to that river.

My brother's leg slipped and he fell into that river.

As soon as he fell into the river, he became a normal person, which means non-infected.

I was happy to see my brother back all well. Then the girl said that it is not a natural river.

It was a man-made river formed by the help of those big containers in that big room.

So, I remembered, that my brother cured just after falling down in the river, and the river is so big that it can adjust more than 500 people.

So, I thought to take a risk, and I told Adira (the girl) to give me the keys of the jeep and said sorry in advanced, as I was about to destroy her jeep.

She gave me the key, because she wanted the people to be

cured.

Just after that, she and my brother went to hide somewhere and I went to the railway track were all the zombies were present.

I beeped the horn to attract them,

they all got attracted towards me and quickly rantowards me,

I drove the jeep at their walking speed so that they could come with me.

I made them reach the river by the way of forest, so that they all could come easily behind me.

I reached the river, and opened the windows of the jeep by which I could come out of it in the river.

But, by mistake, I drove the jeep onto a ramp-like stone, due to which the jeep went to the other side of the river.

Still, it was the luck of the girl, that her jeep did not drown in the water and all the infected people were cured…

It was a big win…

But I had some injuries

Everyone was cured; I was also well.

But, In the temple, Adira saw a camera, she asked that of whom is it…

It was not mine, and not even of my brother.

To check of whom camera it was, we saw the photos inside it. There was a photo of any scientist, Dr. D.L. Sian.

There were some videos, we saw it and got a big shock.

That scientist had invented this deadly disease. We were very angry.

We went to police station and said everything that happened, and about the scientist as per the camera.

Just after listening to us, they started searching for him.

Later in 3-4 days, the

scientist was caught, and he told why did he do all this.

His main purpose was that, he wanted to take control in all over the country, followed by a state, and after that, to all over the world.

He was punished...

LIFE PRISON.

And now, me and my brother could go back home.

Adira with her brother, who was infected before, could also go home back

ALIVE DUMMY STATUES

Chapter 1

In the Market

A family came in a mall; 2 children, their parents, and their grandparents.

They came in 2 separate cars. The children were naughty, they used to run here and there every time whenever they were outside.

In the mall, when their parents went to buy things, and they started playing Hide and Seek.

Their father was busy in buying a new mobile, so, their mother thought to play with her children.

Children's grandparents were helping their father to buy his mobile.

So, the children's mother started counting and the children went to hide behind a dummy statue. But one statue waved his hand, so the first bother thought that the second brother was trying to scare

him, so he ignored it and both of them kept hiding there only.

Their mother, by mistake forgot them and her eyes went on some beautiful jewelleries.

After sometime, when father had taken his item, they all went by

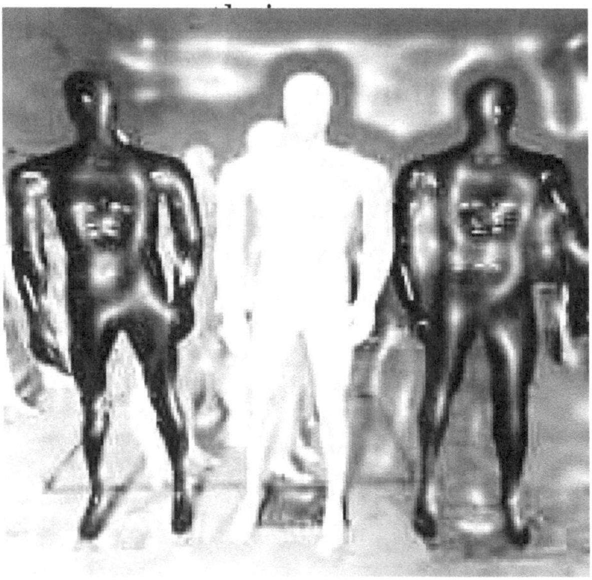

In the car, mother and father were talking about their children, mother thought that may be the children were with their grandparents, so they kept quiet.

Whereas, their grandparents thought that the children must be with their parents.

This misunderstanding is going to give a big problem to the family later.

Chapter 2
In the House

In the house when everyone sat for dinner, Father asked that where were the children.

So, the mother called them.

They were not coming, so the mother went to the children's room angrily, but she couldn't find them.

She told this to everyone, all the family members and the servants started searching for them.

No one could find them,

everyone was confused, and thought what to do.

So, the mother remembered that she was playing with them and the children went to hide and thought that she had made a very big mistake.

She told this to her husband, listening about what happened, he called the shop owner immediately.

But the owner rejected quickly to open the shop and explained that the shop is cursed, if anyone goes into it after 12 am, he or she never comes back, as they are converted into a statue.

He advised them to go to a sorcerer.

When they went to the sorcerer, the

sorcerer said that they had time till 3:31 am, if the children could defend the statues that had come alive and gave them some type of ashes to throw on any one of the statues, which could stop all the statues that have come alive.

But they could use the ashes after 3 am only!!

Chapter 3
Children stuck in the mall

The children were scared in the mall as everyone had gone and the children were not able to see anything properly as it was dark.

One brother saw a statue coming in front of him with a knife. He told the other brother and they both ran immediately.

Some other statues also started walking and some horrible noise was coming from inside, which made the children more scared.

Quickly, one brother took a rod from the shelf and threw it on one dummy statue which had knife. The rod went through the chest of statue and blood was coming out.

The children were confused that how blood was coming out.

At that time, every statue's mouth got opened, their teeth were big and sharp, stained with blood. It was scary for the children.

They quickly started running round and round so that they could confuse the statues.

But during the run, one brother's leg slipped and he fell down.

To defense the brother who fell down, the other brother started kicking on the foot of the statues who came towards them.

He did this until the brother who fell down, stood.

When the brother stood, they both started running again and, in the middle, found a place to hide and hid there.

One brother's eyes became watery
because of fear.
He wanted to go to his mother, but
the other brother gave him
courage.

Although he was also scared from
inside and his heartbeat was fast.
He was making himself ready to
fight with those dummies if any of
them comes towards them, and was
waiting for his parents to come.

Chapter 4
Parents in the mall

On the other hand, their parents broke the gate and came inside the mall and immediately started searching their children.

But there, the children were seen by one statue and was coming towards them to kill them, but the boy started hitting on the statues by a rod to
defense himself and was running with his brother.

Unfortunately, some other statues came in front of them and they were stuck.

...Whereas the parents saw them, and came running towards them, and started pushing the statues, the time was 2:59, and they could use the ashes after 3.

One dummy attacked on father, and father fell down with blood coming out of his arms.

Seeing this, mother saw the time, and the time was 3:02 am, which was a luck for her, and even for her family.

She took the ashes and threw on a dummy statue. All the dummies started cracking and got vanished.

Everyone was safe.

They all slept there because of tiredness.

After 3:30, one by one, staffs came.

And the family woke up. Their eyes were red as they were sleepy, the children were yet

sleeping.

It was the day that they could never forget. They all went back and lived a happy life.

HAUNTED HOTEL

Chapter 1
With Friends

Me and my friends had planned to

go out for a trip.

We were 8 friends for the trip to Goa, 9 days trip. We booked 10 tickets to go from train, 8 for each one and 2 for our luggage.

We all were excited to go, as it was a group trip.
Yuvan and Amogh, my best friends, started searching for the places to visit, on their mobiles, whereas, I was taking full joy of outside.

Other five, Aryan, Piyush, Smaran, and Aditya, Kiyansh were sitting in different coach.

The train started and the time was 8:45 am.

To reach Goa, the train takes 28 hours as written in google.

Yuvan started playing game and Amogh slept on his berth. I also joined Yuvan for playing game.

I took out my phone and opened free fire and challenged Yuvan for a custom match.

After sometime, Smaran came to our berth and sat beside me, and asked what we both were doing, we said that we were playing FF.

So, he took a look to our gameplay.

I was having headache, so I gave my mobile to Smaran and went to sleep.

They both, Smaran and Yuvan played for almost 1hour.

My mobile's battery was 12% left. So, I plugged in my mobile to charge it and saw outside.

It was drizzling, "such a comfortable and cool weather" I thought.

But just after that I remembered, where would we stay for several days, so quickly, I opened my mobile and started searching for a hotel, I found a hotel and booked 4 rooms, thinking of 2 in each room.

It was booked, and then our lunch came,

"Ah! Tasty chicken and rice, I became fan of it"

It was literally very tasty; we all couldn't even waste any of the thing.

In the evening meal we got tea and some snack, in the dinner we again got chicken and rice with 2 chapatis.

It was very tasty and the serving was good. We allslept due tiredness, in addition, the train was 2 hours late so we got extra time to sleep which was good for me.

We arrived in the station, so I immediately woke up but all my other friends were sleeping except Amogh as his sleep was over.

We both made them all awake, and went out ofthe train.

Then by bus we went to the Hotel. There were only 2 people in the hotel,

a manager and a staff.

We were shocked but we were in hurry, as we were tired and hungry and wanted to be freshened first.

We quickly went to our room but the manager told me that...

Chapter 2
In the hotel

But the manager told me that, not to open the gate at night, I could not understand that why did he say this.

Although I ignored him and quickly went in ourroom,

took a bath and got ready for shopping as Piyush and Smaran wanted some clothes,

taking the opportunity, I bought two big pizzas, and we all ate it with joy.

We divided our rooms, I had to sleep with Yuvan,Amogh with Smaran, Piyush with Aditya and Kiyansh with Aryan.

In the room, me and Yuvan were playing FF onceagain, and in talk, I told him about the thing the manager told me.

Just after that, someone started knocking the doornon-stop, I thought that the manager told me about this only, I just told it to Yuvan, so Yuvan also did not open

the door,

but what about the others, so I quickly told this toAryan, Kiyansh, Amogh and Smaran through calling them, but by mistake, I did not tell this toPiyush and Aditya.

Suddenly knocking stopped, and then we could listen the voice of knocking of the door of Aditya, I quickly called Piyush but he was not answering, so, I called Aditya whose mobile was switched off, what could I do now.

Just after that, “Aaah! Help….!, Help me….!!” Voice of Piyush, and Aditya was also screaming. I quickly went out of the door and a lightening type of reflection, which had the speed of a bullet train, actually faster than it, went from the front of my face, because of which my eyes closed and I was not able to open my eyes for almost 10-15 minutes, when I opened my eyes, my friends were in front of me, and my eyes were red and paining.

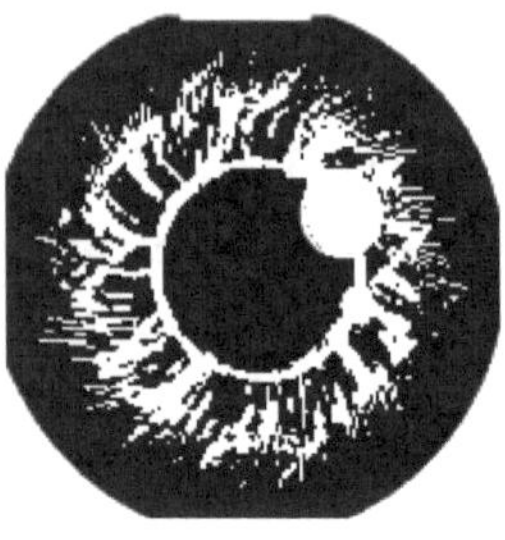

"Who was at the door?" we all were thinking that only, "what to do now?" We were scared about Piyush and Aditya. Smaran was thinking of going back, but we all were thinking about our friends, we all were confused that who was there at night.

How did the manager know about the same, so, to ask about it, we went to the manager, he was trying to ignore us.

There was no way, I had to shout at him and hold his collar.

He was scared, and lastly, he told us about everything. He said that:-

"He is a spirit, of 19 years, He died in this hotel only, he had his younger brother, he was only of 13 years when he died.

Everyone says that they died by fighting with each other, but actually, they were killed by someone. His face was undefined.

The two brothers were dead, but the next day, no one could find their

dead body, only I know where is their body now,

Their body is buried under this hotel, as, that day a call came to me, the person gave me threat of killing my family.

He gave me a condition,

If I did not bury those dead bodies beneath the hotel, he could have killed my family, I was scared, that is why I buried them.

Because of that, both brothers' spirits are roaming in this hotel to take revenge, as, no one is searching for the killer, and have told the lie in front of
everyone that they both died because of fighting and hitting each other.

By kidnapping the people, they take the people to their place where they keep the people in a big cage and take energy from everyone so that they could not attain salvation.

Because they want to take revenge."

Chapter 3
Where are they?

We understood everything… but what about our friends? Where were they?

We asked the manager that where do the spirits keep the kidnapped people.

We were scared for them.

The manager told us that they live and keep the kidnapped people in the basement. No one goes there as everyone is scared that the spirits would kill them, as once a staff went inside and could not come back.

Thinking for our friends, we all 6 went there inside.
Without being scared.

We were going inside, it was literally not looking like a basement, it was looking like we were going under the earth where groundwater is present,
many types of plants were also present there, withmoist cliffs.

Suddenly, A big flow of water came

with greatpressure and hit us. I was in the back, so I was saved but what about all others, where had theygone!! I couldn't find them.

They didn't know to swim, how would they survive, I thought.

Then, I heard all of them screaming to help them. Where I again saw that reflection of anything that Isaw at night.

Then I understood that the reflection is of one of the brothers' spirits.

I was scared and hopeless, as I was alone, in the dark place. I didn't want to go back as; they all were my friends.

I was stuck, I had the only way -> "to swim and go to the other side." But I was scared that if the spirit would take me with him.

Then I thought that if the spirit would take me to his place, I would be able to escape from there with my

friends.
It could help me a lot.

So, I quickly jumped into the water and acted as if I was searching

Just after that, the reflection came back, andstarted pulling my leg. His face was very muchscary, and blood was coming out of his eyes.

Ignoring it, I tried to see the way from which he wastaking me, but he was so fast that I could not see anything and my eyes were starting to pain.

I closed my eyes to have relax but part of a cliff hit my head, because of which, very much blood started coming out of my head and I got fainted.

Chapter 4
Where am I?

When I got consciousness, I was back with my friends. We were in a room which had no doors and no windows, it was very much smelly and not ventilated.

No one was there except us.

After sometime a boy came… he said Piyush to go with him, I asked "why?". The boy looked at me, and started staring me continuously, his eyes were becoming red, his ears started to grow, his teeth became big and he screamed in a tone which made us shout in fear.

He raised his one hand, by that I was automaticallystanding up, as if anyone was holding my neck.
I was unable to breathe properly, and my tongue was coming out as if I was about to die.

My friends were trying to make me sit down but Iwas not able.

My neck was paining and I was almost dead, as I was unable to breath.

At last Aryan pulled me hard so that I could sit down

I was able to breathe now.

I couldn't understand that why had God make uscome here. I was becoming emotional and told myself goodbye.

But Amogh said that we can try to escape from there. He tried to motivate us. But I was becoming hopeless because of the previous scene.

It was unforgettable!!

So, we made a circle and started to plan to escape from here.

Unfortunately, they chose me to check the way.

I am always a scapegoat.

I, in fear, went outside the room, and kept walking in the search of the way. In the way I saw stairs, which could be our escape route, so I went through it where I found sunlight coming inside.

I was right, it was our escape route.

But just after that, I listened a terrifying sound which made me still and scared.

I wanted to go back to my friends, but how could I go?

After some seconds, someone started coming, whose shadow was visible. As per the shadow - that person had big ears, as of an elephant, he also had big nails, I thought that this is the same boy who held my neck.

It was scary, as this time he would probably kill me.

There was no place of hiding.

This is my best policy, of hiding in front ghosts.

Fortunately, I saw a trapdoor beneath my foot, not thinking of anything, I went inside it.

Such a smelly area!!!

I was going ahead, because I was thinking that the boy could come in.

The smell was over after sometime, but the place I had reached, was moist, I was scared that if the water comes out once again.

I was going ahead, where I saw sunlight again, Ithought it was a second route.

But… No.

Aditya had opened torch.

The place was where we were sitting, there was atrapdoor, through which we could come out easily.

I should have come from there, as shortcut is always a better way.

I knocked on the trapdoor, because of which Aditya got scared.

He looked inside, he saw me, and exclaimed
"Aarav!!" he asked me that how did I come there.

He was confused, but he opened the trapdoor, and I came out. Smaran was happy and was saying
that most probably I had found the way to go out. They all were happy, and came in confidence of getting out.

But just after that another boy came, he was ofaround 20 years.

I remembered that the manager

said that there was one boy who was of 19 years, most probably, he was the one who is 19 years old.

I thought, he is the one who was outside when I found in the way.

I thought that he had come to kill me. But he disappeared, what was he trying to do, we didn'tknow... Although we were scared, obviously if all this happens, everyone's pant gets wet...

He appeared once again, so I, in anger, took a rod kept in the corner, and threw on him, he was saved because he disappeared at an accurate time!!!

(His reflexes!!)
He was laughing like a big monster; his purpose was like of killing me. He disappeared and appeared directly in front of me, he had whole black eyes, from which blood was coming out, he was whole white and his teeth were like something terrible.

He picked me up without touching me, and threw me just like I am any object, not a living being.

My circumstances were not of standing; my backache had started, "Help!" I screamed in pain.

None of my friends was having strength to help me in front of the ghost.

I was lying on the floor in pain, I was almost crying,"why did we come here? I want to die now" I said to myself emotionally.

I had less hopes of

being survived. This

time, Amogh was

also quiet.

I was unable to stand, although the ghost had gone, Smaran and Piyush helped me to stand, I had

become weak from inside.

Aditya said that we should get out from there, by the trapdoor.

We all agreed.

We all went down from the trapdoor; they all holdtheir nose tightly because of the smell.

But in the way…

Chapter 5
In the way

In the way, everything was same, but we could hear some horrible noises. We were scared that if the brothers would see us, we would be finished up.

We all were going, where the boy came back. This time, he was with a sword, it was like it was dipped in a tub filled with blood, it was a red sword. (red -> blood)

We were scared, that he would kill us, as we were free-handed, and he was armed.

Although we were 8 and he was 1. So, we tried to kill him with his own sword.

But we could not even touch him, just like he was an air.

We could only touch his sword, but we could not take it from him as his grip was hard.

Then I remembered that when I threw the rod on that 19 years old brother, he was pushed slightly back with the force of rod, he was safe because he disappeared at right time.

So, I kicked on the hand of the boy as hard as I could. He, in pain, threw the sword, then Aryan picked it up and was about to end the boy.

But I stopped him. “As of the story of the brothers, they both were innocent, they were killed intentionally by someone.”

Hearing it, the boy fell down on my legs and saidthank you.

I was shocked, because first time any ghost fell down on my legs.

Also, now we could touch him, he

took us to his brother. But I told him to say his brother not to kill me.

He told me not to worry.

When we went to his brother, we saw his brothercrying, he was crying because he wanted to go to his parents.

Amogh told him not to cry. Just after that the boy said that we became his friends, in addition, he said that we could help them by telling everyone and their parents, that they did not die due to fighting with each other, the manager killed them.

Listening this, we became puzzled,

what were we listening from the boys!! We were literally confused...

How did that manager kill them. We thought that he is good man

Chapter 6
The truth

Then they told the truth...

"Actually,

In the starting days of the hotel, this hotel was veryfamous, and many tourists came in this hotel.

The manager of this hotel was earlier the friend of our father.

But, once they started fighting due to some reasons,their fight grew and it came in the form of violence, (killing).

They both wanted to kill each other's family.

Our father was trying to go out of the matter but the manager, namely Raman, was trying to take our father in the matter.

Our father was angry and one day, he slapped Raman uncle in front of the public.

Because of which he thought that he was ashamed in front of everyone.

He thought to kill us due to the loss

of his ego; he could not kill our father as there was a tight security around our father.

After some months, Raman uncle started this hotel, RAMANDAS HOTEL.

Our father didn't know about it, he thought tosend us to Goa as my younger brother wanted to come here.

Our parents thought that I am big enough to handle everything so he sent me with my brother to Goa.

I booked a room in this hotel.

When we came in this hotel, Raman uncle recognized me, but I could not remember him.

That day, at night around 1 am, he came in front of our room and rang the bell.

I opened the gate, he quickly, with a knife attacked on my stomach, my brother was scared

and screamed “Bhaiyaa!!!”

I fell down on the floor, and Raman uncle went to my brother and attacked with knife on his chest, he died, and after that, Raman uncle, once again
attacked on my stomach where he already hadattacked.

Then, some of his friends and some staffs came inside, they started kicking me, I was in pain, whereas, Raman uncle took my brothers body to basement, and buried him there.

I was also buried with him, even when I was alive.

I was buried alive!!

And now we both brothers are roaming in this hotel to kill him.

But we are unable to kill him as he has worn a thread on his wrist which makes him safe from being killed by us.

We do not kill anyone for their energy.

We only kill all those people who were involved inkilling us. Those were the staffs, and 3 other people.

Those three people were Raman uncle's friends.

I have killed 2 staffs, but the 3 people are not killed yet.

I hope that you would help us to make them gobehind the bars.

Please help us, we will be grateful to you."

After listening to them, we all got emotional, theywere cheated, we promised to help them,

and went to the manager and said the manager, that he could not lie once again, we were literally angry with him, we wanted to kill him, but Kiyansh had called the police.

The manager called his friends, they were 11 in total (including Raman) !

We were 8, They were 11.

But it was not the time to scare, as 2 more were with us.

Chapter 7
Fight

Amogh and Kiyansh ran to attack them, where, I and Yuvan, threw a table on them, they were not stopping. In addition, they all were body builders!!

I kicked a grand-fatty man, he fell down by holding my leg, I fell down, but Yuvan helped me,

In the other hand, Aryan, Smaran, Aditya and Piyush were hitting everyone by table legs...

The manager was trying to go away, but the twobrothers pushed him inside. He fell down on chair, so, being opportunist, I threw another chair on him.

Whereas Yuvan had made the fatty fully injured that he was not able to move.

We all made everyone so much injured that no onecould not even move.

The manager was scared, and the brothers were about to kill him, as, fortunately, manager's thread had opened... "Noo!!!" Aryan screamed, in addition I said that they must not kill him, as, if they would kill him, then we would become the

killers, would be prisoned and later we will be hanged.

They both understood my talk... we were theirfriends, that's why they didn't want us to be in jail.

After sometime, police came, they saw

us and thebrothers standing. They thought that we were thesuspected people.

But then the brothers said that we had not done anything, they said that the manager and those 10body builders were the criminals.

They added that they had killed them both.

The police became confused, thinking that the brothers are standing in front of them, even afterthey were saying that the manager and those people had killed them both.

They said that they wanted evidence.

We said that they both are already dead, they arespirits that you are able to see.

So, to proof it, the brothers said the police to touchthem.

The policeman wasn't able to touch them.

So, they confusingly agreed.

After that, one brother told the whole story to thepolice, and the next day, the manager and those people were arrested and later hanged after the hearing in the court...

The End

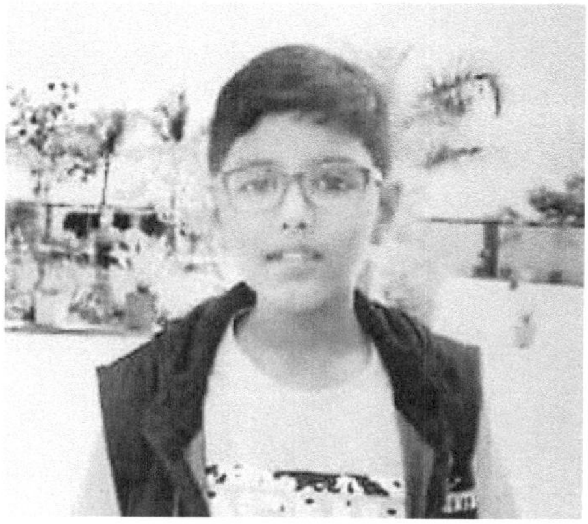

I am Aarav Mehta, a 13-years-old boy of class 8th in Ahlcon Public School situated in Delhi, Mayur Vihar, Phase-1.

It's my first Horror book.

I like to read and make stories through my powerful imaginations.

This book is made because of full support and love from my lovely mother, Adv. Gunjan Mehta and my pillar of strength like father, Adv. Amrendra Kumar Mehta.

I want to become an Advocate of Supreme Court of India, just like my father, and want to try my best, so that all the poor people can attain their justice.

New Arrival

Arriving soon

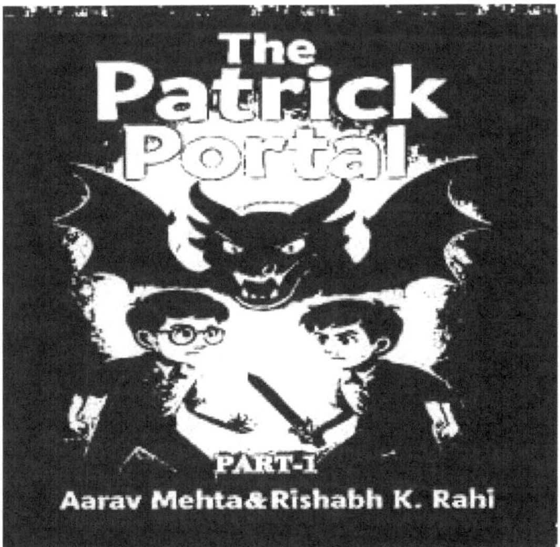